Underwater Adventure!

Based on the original stories created by
Ian Whybrow and Adrian Reynolds

PUFFIN BOOKS
Published by the Penguin Group: London, New York,
Australia, Canada, India, Ireland, New Zealand and South Africa
Penguin Books Ltd, Registered Offices: 80 Strand, London WC2R 0RL, England

puffinbooks.com

First published 2009
1 3 5 7 9 10 8 6 4 2

Made and printed in China
ISBN: 978–0–141–50243–4

Harry and Nan were at the beach, and Harry was making a very special sandcastle. He found the perfect shell to go on top. "That looks great!" Harry said to his dinosaurs.

But his dinosaurs weren't happy. "What's wrong?" Harry asked.

"Sorry, Harry," said Taury. "But we just don't like this new bucket."

"We like our old blue bucket best!" grumbled Pterence.

"Don't worry," Harry reassured his dinosaurs,
"Nan bought this pink one for us to use at the beach,
so we don't get our blue one all sandy and wet."

Just then, they realized
that Harry's special shell
had disappeared.

"There it is!" yelled
Sid. They all raced
down the beach to
try to catch it.

"My shell has run away!" Harry cried.

"Maybe it's a hermit crab," suggested Nan. "Sometimes they live inside shells and rock pools."

"I wish I could follow it into the sea," said Harry.

"You're a little boy, Harry, not a fish!" said Nan.

"I know somewhere we can swim underwater safely," said Taury. "In Dino World!"

Luckily Nan had brought Harry's blue bucket to the beach too, just in case.

One, two, three . . . JUMP!

"I'm on my way to . . .

In Dino World they had real diving suits and a submarine.

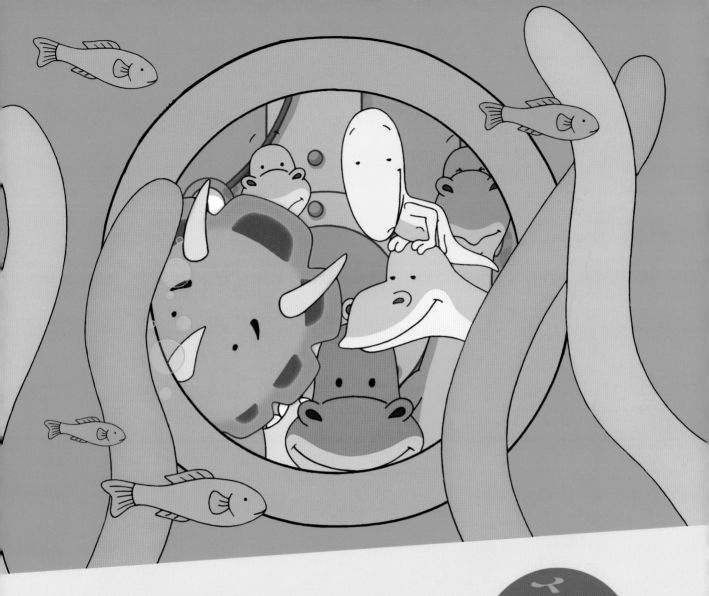

They whooshed through the waves
and saw lots of amazing sea creatures.
Then Taury spotted Harry's shell,
scuttling along the ocean floor!

"Quick!" cried Harry, "let's follow it!"
But they couldn't swim fast enough ... until some friendly seahorses helped them.
"Whee!" said Taury. "This is great!"

Finally they caught up with the shell.
"It's a hermit crab, just like Nan said!"
Harry exclaimed.

But the hermit crab was very sad. He had outgrown his shell, and now it was so tight he couldn't get out! "I should have found a new shell ages ago," he groaned.

Harry and his dinosaurs tried to
help. They pulled and pulled, but the
hermit crab was still stuck.

Then they had a very good idea.
They crept away and hid, and then . . .

... they jumped out and shouted "BOO!"

"Oooh!" cried the hermit crab, jumping right out of his shell.

"That's better!" he said, and wriggled all his legs about happily.

Then they tried to find him a new shell to live in.
They brought him lots of shells to try, but none of them
were quite right.

"Too small ..."
said Hermit Crab.

"Too many bits on it ...

... not really my colour!"

"Oh," he sighed. "I don't think I'll ever find a new home."
Harry thought for a little while.
"I know!" he said. "Come with me . . ."

"You can borrow my bucket," said Harry. "It's just the right size."

The hermit crab was delighted with his new home. He scuttled up and down very proudly. "Thank you, Harry!" he said.

Soon it was time for Harry and his dinosaurs to go. Before they left, the hermit crab gave Harry his old shell. "I don't need it any more!" he chuckled.

Harry showed Nan his shell.
"It's perfect!" she said.

Nan helped Harry put the shell on his castle.

"What do you think?" Harry asked his dinosaurs.
   But they didn't answer. They were far too busy settling
back into their nice blue bucket!